Animals and The New Zoos

PATRICIA CURTIS

LODESTAR BOOKS

Dutton • New York

to Patrick William Robbins

Library of Congress Cataloging-in-Publication Data

Curtis, Patricia, 1923–
    Animals and the new zoos / Patricia Curtis.—1st ed.
      p. cm.
    Includes index.
    Summary: Describes the animals of the world's basic habitats
(grasslands, deserts, woodlands, rain forests, cold regions) and how
"better" zoos in this country are trying to exhibit the animals in
environments like their natural ones.
    ISBN 0-525-67347-4
    1. Zoos—Juvenile literature. 2. Zoo animals—Juvenile literature.
3. Open-air zoos—Juvenile literature. 4. Zoos—United States—
Juvenile literature. 5. Open-air zoos—United States—Juvenile
literature. [1. Animals. 2. Zoo animals. 3. Zoos.]
I. Title.
QL76.C87 1991
590'.74'4—dc20   90-45748
                                   CIP
                                   AC

Published in the United States by Lodestar Books, an affiliate of
Dutton Children's Books, a division of Penguin Books USA Inc.
Published simultaneously in Canada by McClelland & Stewart, Toronto

Editor: Virginia Buckley

Designer: Keithley and Associates

Printed in Hong Kong   First Edition   10 9 8 7 6 5 4 3 2 1

Contents

Acknowledgments

I owe special thanks to Karen Asis, director of public relations for the American Association of Zoological Parks and Aquariums, who readily helped me with information and gave me the benefit of her deep understanding of animals.

I also wish to thank my friends Vicki Dennison, an expert researcher, and Jane Sapinsky, a skilled photographer, for their patient interest and professional help.

I was fortunate to have knowledgeable help and counsel from David Herbet, former director of captive wildlife for the Humane Society of the United States and formerly a keeper at the Bronx Zoo. I'm especially grateful to the Humane Society for the use of certain photographs.

Thanks also to Kim Hastings of the International Species Information System; Mike Morgan of the National Zoo, Smithsonian Institution; Reg Hoyt of the Phoenix Zoo; Pam French of the Central Park Zoo; and to the zoos listed at the back of the book, which generously sent me photographs and information.

Animals and the New Zoos

In the past, zoos were places where wild animals were confined in bare cages. You might see a tiger, for instance, whose natural home was the rich, dense jungle but whose home in the zoo was a concrete cage that had maybe a tree trunk and a rock for atmosphere. Zoos tried to collect as many different species of animals as possible—one elephant, one gorilla, one antelope, and so on. As a result, even animals who normally live in families or groups were confined by themselves. They had nothing to do but sleep, sit around, or pace back and forth, in full view of the public who gawked at them and sometimes teased them. Often, animals died from improper care or sheer loneliness. There were no signs or programs that explained the animals or their role in the natural ecosystems of the earth. The zoo was no more than a freak show.

Most zoos today are still like that.

However, many have begun to create exhibits that imitate the animals' natural habitats. Some zoos are building total ecosystems, with trees, plants, soil, water, temperature, and humidity that are much the same as in the animals' wild homes. In these zoos, creatures of different species live and interact much as they do in the wild. They can move freely about and lead almost normal lives.

Traditionally, zoos acquired new animals, or replaced those that died, by buying animals caught in the wild. Hunters went to places where wild animals lived freely, captured whatever animals they could, tied them up, put them in boxes, and shipped them to animal dealers. Many animals died from fear or careless treatment. Then, those animals that survived were sold to zoos, circuses, private collectors—whoever would buy them.

If a zoo tried to acquire new animals by breeding, it was assumed that simply putting a male and female together in the same cage would result in offspring. What usually happened was that the two animals either ignored or tried to kill each other.

Today, zoo managers know that in order for animals to thrive in captivity, and especially to mate successfully, they must live as they do in the wild. Some animals, especially males, are solitary by nature. But most live in pairs of their own choosing, or in families, bachelor or female groups, herds, troops, packs, or other combinations. In good zoos, these differences are known and respected, and animals are kept accordingly.

In the past, infant animals born in zoos were almost always automatically taken from their mothers and raised by humans. Today, they are usually

A once-powerful jaguar leads a dreary life, imprisoned in a bare cage.

In zoos that provide natural habitats, animals like this gorilla family
can behave normally.

raised by their mothers and are better off for it. The great majority of the
animals you now see in zoos were born in captivity.

When you visit one of the better zoos, not only can you see animals from
all over the world behaving much as they would in their wild habitats, but
the exhibits also provide information about them and their environments.

Once in a while, you may have to be patient in order to catch a glimpse of
some of the animals, for in a humane and appropriate zoo environment,
they may not always be easy to see. They may be resting in privacy in their
den, burrow, tree, or shrubbery. Some zoo visitors complain about this, for
they think the animals should be constantly on view, as they are in a bare
cage. But if you truly like and understand animals, you'll be glad they are
comfortable in a good habitat and can behave normally.

Alone in a corner of its rusty cage at a run-down zoo, a gorilla sits in total despair.

In the United States, zoos and other animal exhibits are required to be licensed by the Department of Agriculture. There are about 750 licensed zoos and aquariums. To be licensed, zoos are supposed to exhibit animals in reasonably good environments. But the trouble is, there is no way the Department of Agriculture can or will enforce all the licensing laws among so many zoos. And a lot of zoos are unwilling or unable to spend the money to upgrade their exhibits, so the animals suffer and visitors are cheated.

In 1972, a group of zoo professionals formed the American Association of Zoological Parks and Aquariums (AAZPA). This organization sets standards and guidelines for the keeping of captive wild animals and educates professionals on zoo management and animal care. AAZPA standards are much higher than those of the Department of Agriculture. A zoo must measure up in order to become an accredited member of the AAZPA.

At present, 150 zoos and aquariums in North America are accredited by AAZPA. That's not very many, among 750. But every year, a few more zoos have improved enough to be accepted for AAZPA membership.

One program sponsored by this organization is the Species Survival Plan (SSP), established to save some of the most endangered species. An endangered species is one whose population in the wild has fallen so low that it is in danger of becoming extinct. When a species' ecosystem is significantly changed by natural causes, such as a flood, or more likely by human activity, such as cutting down a forest, the species suffers. If the animals try to move to an ecosystem that's greatly different, they are

Jane Sapinsky

In a zoo's lush rain forest, a black leopard stretches on a limb before seeking privacy in the greenery.

unable to adapt and will die out. Many species, animals and plants, are being lost forever as we humans increasingly take over the planet for ourselves.

At present, about 130 of the best zoos in the United States and in several other countries are cooperating in efforts to keep fifty-four chosen species from dying out. While not all endangered creatures can be saved, one goal of the SSP is to increase healthy populations so that eventually they can be released back into protected natural habitats.

Unfortunately, the reserves that most nations have set aside for their wildlife make up a total of only 1 percent of the earth's land areas. Usually, the reserves are simply land that nobody wants, not critical habitat desperately needed by wildlife. Also, many reserves are too small to support enough animals to keep a species healthy. Some zoos are trying, through excellent exhibits and educational programs, to make people aware of the necessity of preserving not just endangered species but also natural ecosystems in the wild. A few maintain protected reserves for wildlife in other countries. The New York Zoological Society (Bronx Zoo), for instance, supports seventy-five reserves around the world, an important step.

This book is divided into five of the earth's most representative land ecosystems. The animals are grouped together according to their natural habitats within those ecosystems, so that you'll read about them as you might see them exhibited in the better zoos. At a zoo's rain forest exhibit, for example, you'll see many creatures of that ecosystem; similarly, you'll find rain forest animals described together in this book.

It is important to know how animals live in the wild so when you see them in a zoo you'll be able to tell if they are comfortable and able to lead lives that are reasonably normal for them. If the exhibits are good, you'll learn a great deal about both the animals and their natural habitats.

Animals of the Grasslands and Savannas

The ecosystems of the earth do not have boundaries like states or nations; they blend gradually from one to the other. The grassland and savanna ecosystems lie between the deserts or semideserts and the various kinds of forests. Grasslands are generally flat or gently rolling, with few trees. The grasslands of the United States may also be called prairies or plains. The huge plains of Russia are called steppes. Savannas are more parklike, with mixed trees and open, grassy areas. Parts of eastern Africa are savannas.

Grasslands and savannas are the home of the herbivores, those animals who eat grass, leaves, and other vegetation. They are also the home of many carnivores, predatory animals whose diet is mainly herbivores; and also many omnivores, who eat just about everything.

Herbivores include mammals with hoofs, such as deer, antelopes, goats, sheep, and horses, who survive by being alert and able to run for their lives when chased by predators. The predators or carnivores have to be strong and fast enough to catch them. Lions, tigers, and dogs are carnivores, as are the raptors, meat-eating birds such as eagles, hawks, and owls.

Good zoos keep their grassland animals in enclosures that are much like their wild habitats, except, of course, without predators.

There is one grassland animal that you'll see only in zoos because it is extinct in the wild—the Asian wild horse. It has an interesting history. In 1881, a Russian explorer named Nikolai Przewalski (pronounced Prez-wall-ski) was traveling in a remote part of Mongolia when he came across a herd of very unusual wild horses. They were golden tan and quite small and heavy, with stiff, upright, black crests instead of manes. Unknown to Europeans, they had apparently lived on those vast, unexplored steppes for thousands of years. Scientists who began to study them concluded that these animals were the ancestors of all modern horses.

Wild animals are sometimes named after the persons who first identified them for science, and so these horses were originally called Przewalski's horses. Now, they are usually referred to as Asian wild horses or Mongolian wild horses, to identify their habitat. They have never been domesticated or used for work or riding. They are the only true *wild* horses on earth.

The American mustangs, some of whom still live free in a few western states, are called wild horses, but they are actually *feral* horses. Feral means domestic animals that were once owned but have gone wild. The mustangs are the descendants of various kinds of domestic horses that escaped or were turned loose when the West was being settled.

Today, there are only around 850 Asian wild horses, all in zoos and private collections. However, they are being studied and bred under the Species Survival Plan (SSP). All the Asian wild horses in SSP cooperating zoos are filed on a computer with details of their age, sex, and characteristics. Then, the cooperating zoos share information about their horses and lend or swap them from time to time for breeding. The hope for the future is that several healthy herds can be reintroduced to their original home or to a comparable wilderness area.

Horses in the wild live in harems consisting of a stallion, his mares, and their offspring. When the stallion's sons reach maturity, he drives them out of the harem. They go off and live by themselves, or team up with another bachelor or two, until they can lure some fillies away from other

Scientists believe the Asian wild horse, an ancient and almost extinct species,
is the ancestor of the modern horse.

harems and start their own. Zookeepers are alert to this natural pattern and keep Asian wild horses in groups consisting of a stallion and his harem. They watch the maturing colts, and when the stallion begins to harass them, the zookeepers move the young males to pastures of their own, or to other zoos that are cooperating in the SSP.

Among species that live in groups, it is not unusual for the young males to leave, or be driven out, when they become mature. This prevents continual inbreeding among close relatives, which tends to weaken a species.

———

Thousands of different hoofed species graze on the grasslands of the world. One from East Africa, the gerenuk (pronounced jer-a-nuk), belongs to the group of small, graceful, delicate antelopes called gazelles. Male gerenuks weigh only about 115 pounds—that's small, considering that some kinds of antelopes are as big as ponies and can weigh several hundred pounds. Because of its unusually long neck, the gerenuk is sometimes called giraffe-necked. When browsing, it stands up on its hind legs and extends its long neck in order to eat the leaves on the lower branches of trees.

In the wild, gerenuks live together in pairs or in small herds of seven or eight, and a good zoo also keeps them that way. Naturally, when they live in normal herds, they breed. The public loves to see baby animals. But unless a zoo has plenty of room or needs to replace animals that died, or another good zoo wants gerenuks, breeding can, in the end, cause suffering. If the zoo cannot locate another decent zoo that wants them, it may have no choice but to sell the young animals to an animal dealer. The dealer in turn auctions off animals to anybody who will pay the highest price, whether a roadside zoo, circus, research laboratory, or private hunting ranch, where deer and antelopes are especially wanted. Some may be slaughtered and their meat sold to restaurants.

Saint Louis Zoo

It's easy to see why gerenuks are called "giraffe-necked" antelopes.

baby lion barely old enough to leave its mother waits to sold at an animal auction in Cape Girardeau, Missouri.

Will the baby lion end up like this lion in a cramped, filthy cage at a ramshackle Indiana zoo?

Roadside zoos are amateur places set up alongside highways, back roads, or gas stations to attract tourists. The animals are kept in conditions that range from poor to horrible.

Hunting ranches are enormous places where people pay big money to go in and shoot animals for fun. The animals—deer, antelopes, rare goats and sheep, perhaps even bears, zebras, lions, or tigers—are loose, but they can't get away because the ranches are fenced, so a hunter never leaves without a trophy. Even a rare animal like the gerenuk may end up as a stuffed head on the wall of some wealthy person's living room.

Another method zoos may use to cope with surplus animals is to "warehouse" them, keeping them indefinitely in cages in the basements of zoo buildings. Even the best zoos sometimes warehouse surplus animals. Unless a species is being bred in the Species Survival Plan, or there is a demand among good zoos for certain animals, a responsible zoo will separate males from females during breeding season. The Humane Society of the United States has been urging zoos to carefully control the breeding of *all* captive wildlife.

The **pronghorn**, a handsome native of the American western prairies, is the second-fastest animal on earth—only the cheetah, a large spotted cat from Africa and Asia, can run faster. The pronghorn looks much like an antelope, though scientifically it is not exactly one. In the wild, when a pronghorn senses danger, it signals by raising the bushy white hairs on its rump, which other pronghorns can see from a mile away, and they all take off. Few animal predators can even come close to them. But they cannot outrun bullets.

Pronghorns are nomads, so they don't stay year round in one grazing area but keep on the move searching for new grass. They follow the same

Second-fastest animal on earth, this pronghorn buck would be considered a fine trophy by hunters.

migration routes year after year, which may cross either public lands or private ranch lands. The public lands belong to the people of the United States, but our government lets ranchers graze their cattle on them. The ranchers are not allowed to fence those public lands if the fences would interfere with wildlife. However, the ranchers fence their own lands. In many instances, they have put their fences right across the migrating routes the pronghorns use to get to their winter grazing lands. The animals can't cross over, under, or through the fences. So every year, thousands of pronghorns die, piled up against the ranchers' fences.

Only 1 percent of the original herds are left today. At least you can find pronghorns in some western and midwestern zoos.

———

Another animal of the American western grasslands is the **prairie dog**, which, as you can see from the photograph on page 14, isn't a dog at all. It is a rodent, related to the squirrel and about the same size. But when frightened, it gives a sort of bark, like that of a small terrier. It is a favorite animal in many zoos.

Prairie dogs once lived all over the broad plains. They created entire underground prairie dog towns with their burrows. A town could cover hundreds of square miles and include hundreds of millions of inhabitants. In the early morning and evening, the animals spent a lot of time together sitting up on their haunches, never far from the entrances to their burrows. When one of them perceived danger, it would bark to warn the others and pop underground, and all its neighbors would do the same.

Prairie dogs were dinner to such predators as badgers, bobcats, hawks, and eagles. However, the early human settlers of the West killed off most of those predators. So, since prairie dog food—grass, flowers, and roots— was plentiful and predators were few, the result was a population explosion of prairie dogs. Then the ranchers decided that the prairie dogs were destroying the rangeland that they wanted for their cattle. So they poisoned, shot, trapped, gassed, and otherwise killed off most of the prairie dogs. Today, some ranchers with prairie dogs living on their land, especially in

A prairie dog looks like a fat, sturdy squirrel
but has only a short tail.

Even though it's in a naturalistic habitat behind glass
zoo, this meerkat is on guard duty, watching for preda

Colorado, hold annual prairie dog shoots; people who kill for fun are invited to come and slaughter the animals. Zoos seem to be the only places where these once-common small American animals are safe.

A good zoo will keep prairie dogs in a habitat that allows them to dig their underground living space. When the Arizona-Sonora Desert Museum acquired its first prairie dogs, the animals tunneled their way out of the zoo, so now they are confined to an exhibit that's like a concrete swimming pool filled with dirt. At the Phoenix Zoo, they have six feet of dirt contained by chain link fencing. The animals remodel their snug burrows frequently. They are good construction engineers, creating rooms for sleeping, nesting, and storage. The babies are born in the burrows and emerge in the spring.

When their population exceeds their space at a zoo, some may be sold or traded to other zoos that want to start prairie dogs exhibits. They are attractive animals and fun to watch, so at present other zoos want them.

The meerkat is another zoo favorite. This little South African animal is not related to any species of cat, but it is about the size of a small housecat. The early Dutch settlers in South Africa gave it its name. Its closest kin is the mongoose.

Meerkats live in a highly cooperative society. In the wild, they live in burrows as close together as possible, hunt for lizards and insects, share food, hug and groom one another, and help care for one another's babies. In a good zoo, they dig burrows, or burrows are provided for them.

Meerkats don't sit on their haunches, as prairie dogs, squirrels, or rabbits do. They stand, with their short front legs hanging down in front.

Because they live on flat, open land where hawks and other predators can easily spot them, meerkats are in constant danger above ground. But they protect themselves by taking turns doing guard duty! One meerkat is always standing on a mound or perched in a tree, keeping watch. When one guard gets tired, after several minutes or an hour, another member of the group volunteers. Even in a zoo, you'll often see one on guard duty. They don't realize that in the zoo they don't have to worry about predators.

One very efficient predator of the savannas is the African wild dog, also called the African hunting dog or Cape hunting dog. It has a massive head, long legs, sharp teeth, and is about as big as a medium-sized domestic dog.

African wild dogs hunt in packs, chasing their prey, often in relays, until the victim becomes exhausted and the dogs can close in and kill it. But the dogs themselves are relentlessly killed by human hunters, who consider them competitors for antelopes and zebras. Whenever wild animals must compete with people for their food—whether it's prey to kill or land to graze on—in the long run the animals always lose.

In the savannas, African wild dogs live in packs of up to sixty members. They cooperate with one another according to strict and complex rules.

Some pack members are hunters while others stay home and guard the pups in the dens. The hunters bring food to the young, to all nursing mothers, and to those pack members who are too old or injured to hunt for themselves. The pups are fed even when adults have to go hungry. Pack members lick one another's lips as a sign of greeting.

Unlike domestic dogs, these animals are monogamous, which means they stay with one mate for life. Males and females share in taking care of their pups. The one area in which pack members sometimes compete is over pups. Adult females may try to steal one another's offspring, and the poor pups get caught in the middle, dragged back and forth between warring females.

Zoos generally keep African wild dogs in groups of related males. New males won't be accepted into a pack, but females can be introduced for mating. Good zoos manage their African wild dogs in such a way that peace

Cincinnati Zoo/Ron Austing

An African wild dog may not be beautiful, but it is an excellent hunter, devoted parent, and loyal pack member.

is maintained and pups are protected. This is an example of the importance of the knowledge gained by scientists who study animals in the wild. What they learn by patient observation helps zoos know how to take better care of wild animals in captivity.

————

Another African animal, the ostrich, is the biggest bird on earth. It is so heavy that it can't get off the ground to fly. The Masai, or red-necked, ostrich, a native of Kenya and Tanzania, stands eight to nine feet tall and may weigh 220 pounds or more. It is a speedy runner and when chased by a predator can cover twenty-five feet in one stride. But hunting dogs, cheetahs, lions, and leopards kill it for food if they can catch it.

You may have heard that an ostrich buries its head in the sand when frightened. That's a myth. An ostrich does nothing of the sort—it runs, or defends itself by kicking. Its kick is powerful and can even kill a young lion. But loss of habitat takes its toll, and as a result, the species is dwindling in the wild.

Humans have traditionally hunted this bird for its beautiful feathers and plumes. And moreover, in recent years, ostrich farms have been established, both in Africa and in the United States, where the birds are raised like livestock for their plumes and valuable skin. Ostrich skin is used to make handbags and other fine leather goods.

Gladys Porter Zoo

The adult male Masai ostrich, black and white with a pink neck and legs, stands nearly nine feet tall.

When a male ostrich is trying to attract a female for mating, he does a fancy dance in front of her—twirling, bobbing, and spreading his wings. After they mate, they build a big nest together and then take turns sitting on the eggs, which are bigger than grapefruit. When ostrich eggs hatch, all the chicks are escorted everywhere by their parents, who are extremely fierce in protecting them. Even so, only a few chicks live to grow up.

Many zoos have ostriches, including Masai ostriches. In the better-run zoos, they may be kept in large, grassy enclosures with the hoofed animals, such as zebras or antelopes, that they normally live among in the wild.

———

Lord of the African savannas is of course the **elephant**, the largest land mammal on earth. Bull (male) African elephants can weigh six tons— about as much as, say, two pickup trucks. Herds of African elephants, which you might have seen on television, are usually females with young, because that is their normal grouping. Males live apart and join females only for mating.

In recent years, you might have read newspaper or magazine articles, or seen one of the many television documentaries, about the plight of the African elephant. These animals are disappearing in almost all their home- lands, partly beause the African people are taking their habitats for farm- ing, but mostly because poachers are slaughtering them for their ivory tusks. Poachers are men who illegally kill wild animals and sell their skins or other parts of their bodies. Poachers with automatic weapons shoot an estimated two hundred African elephants a day and have already annihi- lated 60 to 90 percent of the herds in several African nations. Poachers even kill baby elephants for their barely formed tusks or leave them to starve after killing their mothers.

Ivory is used to make jewelry and other decorations. People buy such trinkets either because they don't think about how ivory is obtained, or they don't care.

Both the African and the Asian, or Indian, elephants are on the endan- gered species list. The Indian elephants have not been persecuted as much

Samuel, the baby elephant, was born in one zoo and shipped to another, but Tussa, a dominant female, adopted him and mothers him as if he were her own.

by poachers because they have smaller tusks, but they have suffered severe loss of habitat. Zoos are now breeding both species in the SSP.

While the African elephant is difficult to tame and has not been used for work, Asian elephants have been domesticated and used as beasts of burden for thousands of years. The elephants in circuses are Asian and usually females.

The treatment of elephants in captivity is mixed. Elephants, particularly African, can be dangerous; they are powerful and smart. Their handlers control them with an ankus, a long stick with a hook on the end. But handlers claim that they have to establish dominance by discipline, and many rely on harsh methods and cruel punishment. Some use a "hot shot" (a metal bar that gives a painful electric shot). Almost all chain the huge mammals by their feet at night, often for as long as eighteen hours, to keep them from tearing up their barns. If a handler is away or out sick, elephants may be chained for days.

Some years ago, at the Brookfield Zoo, an Asian elephant named Ziggy attacked his trainer during musth, a period of sexual arousal in male elephants when they become extremely difficult. Any experienced handler knows to be especially cautious around a bull elephant during musth. But as punishment Ziggy was put in a cell and left there. Over time, he was more or less forgotten, so he was kept in the cell for *thirty years*. When he was finally unshackled and allowed to come out in a yard, he was so weak he could hardly walk.

In 1988, at the San Francisco Zoo, an Asian elephant named Tinkerbelle hurt two zoo employees who were trying to treat a sore in her mouth. As punishment, she was beaten and given the hot shot. The keepers said they disciplined elephants by what they called "stressing them out"—chaining and hitting the animals until they urinated and defecated from fear.

Also, in 1988, at the famous San Diego Wild Animal Park, a wild-caught African elephant named Dunda, who threatened a keeper, was chained on her belly and beaten over the head with axe handles for two days, under the direction of the chief elephant handler. There was a widespread protest from the public, and even the Department of Agriculture threatened legal action if such punishment was ever repeated.

This sort of treatment may occur at many zoos, behind the scenes where the public can't see. Today, the Brookfield Zoo manages its elephants humanely; yet the handler who ordered Dunda's beating said his practices were standard. Episodes such as these are very troubling to people who care about animals. They raise the question of whether elephants should be kept in zoos at all.

Fortunately, the incidents have also focused attention on the handling of captive elephants and the need to improve their care. Several of the better zoos are remodeling their elephant barns so the animals don't have to be chained at night. The AAZPA has formulated guidelines on the handling of elephants that it hopes all zoos will adopt. If the recommendations are followed, zoo elephants will lead better lives.

Some zoos, such as Woodland Park and the National Zoo, have good reputations for their elephant care. Some follow a hands-off policy with elephants and have few accidents among their handlers. There are handlers who object to the hot shot and do not use it, and who are affectionate toward their animals.

A good elephant exhibit will provide plenty of space for the animals to move around in, shade from the sun, a pool deep enough for the animals to completely submerge in, and a mud wallow so they can cool off by plastering mud over their sensitive skins. In Georgia, where the mud is red, Zoo Atlanta's elephants are often red!

Elephants are expensive to maintain—every day, each one must be fed about a hundred and twenty pounds of hay, grass, grain, and vegetables, with extra vitamins and minerals mixed in. Some zoos grow their herbivores' food themselves. Keepers must keep track of what and how much food every animal eats.

Every zoo elephant has to learn to obey certain commands—for example, it must lift its feet so the handler or veterinarian can check on their condition. At the Woodland Park Zoo, several cooperative Asian elephants give demonstrations of the work they do in their native countries, such as lifting or rolling logs.

But elephants should never be forced to clown around and do silly tricks that make them look ridiculous, because this gives us the wrong message about these majestic and intelligent creatures.

Animals of the Deserts

What all the world's deserts have in common with one another is lack of moisture. They receive very little rainfall. Therefore, vegetation is sparse. Some deserts are hot all year-round, with very high temperatures during the day but cold nights. Other deserts may be hot for only a few weeks in summer. But all are dry.

Nevertheless, a surprising amount of animal life flourishes in the desert—from small mammals and birds to lizards and snakes that can endure extremes of heat and can figure out how to get the water they need. Many desert creatures are nocturnal, which means that they come out to feed or hunt in the cool of the night, and sleep in burrows or shade during the day.

Many of the best zoos with desert animals are located in hot climates where the animals can live outdoors. Other zoos may keep desert animals in exhibits behind glass, where a warm temperature can be maintained.

The **fennec fox** is one desert animal that zoos usually keep in habitats behind glass. This is the world's smallest fox, only about the size of a half-grown kitten. Its enormous ears may look funny, but they're there for a purpose. The fennec hunts at night when its Sahara Desert habitat has cooled off. Its main diet is burrowing insects and mice. It can literally hear

A tiny desert fox with enormous ears, the shy fennec is often kept in a glassed-in habitat at zoos.

the insects moving under the sand and can dig so fast it catches them unawares. It can hear the slightest rustle of mice and pinpoint their location in the dark with its sharp eyesight and hearing.

In the wild, fennecs live in small communities. Their burrows, where they sleep during the day, are sometimes connected. Their creamy color serves to camouflage them well, and their broad paws help them walk and dig in the desert sand.

A good zoo provides either artificial burrows for them, or enough sand for them to dig their own. If you see fennecs in a habitat behind a glass wall or window, never rap or pound on the glass. The sound is magnified inside the habitat and disturbs these shy animals. In fact, this holds true for any animals that are exhibited behind a glass window or wall.

Woodland Park Zoo/Carol Beach

Rare in the wild, rare in zoos, the beautiful little sand cat faces an uncertain future.

The little **sand cat** is another burrowing animal of hot, dry lands. Once found in the deserts of Africa, Arabia, and Pakistan, sand cats were hunted for their pelts. They were also captured in large numbers for the pet trade in the United States and Europe. Many died of respiratory infections because they were improperly cared for. Now, their survival in the wild is uncertain, and they are also rare in zoos.

Sand cats are just a little larger than our pet house cats, with big ears and thick padding of long hair on their footpads to help them walk on hot, shifting desert sand. They don't mew but make a sort of bark.

Like fennecs, these animals are night hunters, crouching in the low desert vegetation and stalking their prey silently, as all cats do. They survive on desert mice, birds, insects, and snakes and can live without drinking water, because they get enough moisture from their prey.

The few zoos that have these highly endangered felines, such as the Woodland Park and the Living Desert, are breeding them in an effort to pull the species back from the brink of extinction.

In its homeland, the elegant **Arabian oryx** (pronounced or-icks) had been hunted to extinction by tribesmen using spears and by Arab princes and European and American sport hunters using trucks, helicopters, high-powered rifles, and machine guns. The hunters would chase the oryxes over long distances till the animals could run no more. Then, as the exhausted beasts collapsed or just stood still, the men would shoot them.

One animal that is gradually being returned to its desert homeland through the Species Survival Plan is the Arabian oryx.

Finally, in 1972, a party of sport hunters shot the last wild Arabian oryx. That would have been the end for this antelope, but fortunately, ten years earlier, conservationists had seen this coming. They had collected a small herd, which they had sent to the Phoenix Zoo, where the climate is hot and dry like the animals' natural habitat. As soon as the oryxes were producing healthy young, and the herd was growing, some were transferred to other warm-climate zoos, such as the Gladys Porter in Texas and the Living Desert in California. Now the animals, their breeding carefully controlled in the Species Survival Plan, have a secure future.

Today, they are being returned, a few small herds at a time, from the zoos to their Arabian homeland. They live on their own in protected reserves where they are not hunted. Oryxes are so well adapted to the desert that they can get enough moisture from the tough grasses they eat. They can go a long time, even years, without drinking water.

Many species of tortoise live in the warm deserts of the world. Tortoises are turtles that live on land. While the ancestors of human beings originated only a few million years ago, the earliest tortoiselike creatures walked the earth with the dinosaurs some two hundred million years ago.

There are over forty species of tortoise, ranging in size from about six inches long to the largest, the Aldabra, whose top shell, the carapace, is about four feet long. Tortoises have no teeth and are exclusively vegetarian. Some live between a hundred and a hundred and fifty years. Though most species of tortoise don't make any sounds except possibly hissing when frightened, the giant species can roar or bellow.

Tortoises are found on every continent except Antarctica. Like all reptiles, they are cold-blooded. Their body temperature is the same as the temperature of their environment. This is why they can't live in climates with temperatures below freezing. The body temperature of warm-blooded creatures such as mammals and birds is independent of their environment.

Dallas Zoo

The handsome radiated tortoise has been saved from extinction
by the Species Survival Plan.

Many species of tortoise are endangered. These animals are slow to reproduce and have almost no defenses against predators, especially humans. They've been killed for food, captured for pets, and suffered habitat loss. If you come across a tortoise in the wild, leave it alone and do not stress it even by picking it up, unless it is in some obvious danger, such as trying to cross a highway. In that case you should move it to safety and let it go.

The radiated tortoise wears a beautiful design on its six-to-eight-inch shell. Its natural habitat is the hot, dry areas of Madagascar, a large island nation off the east coast of Africa. Like all of Madagascar's wildlife, the radiated tortoise is losing its habitat and is highly endangered. Through the Species Survival Plan, zoos are trying to keep this reptile from becoming extinct. In warm-climate zoos, the radiated tortoises live in outdoor enclosures, but in the few northern zoos that have them, they live indoors.

―――――

Among the lizards of hot, dry climates is one fearsome-looking creature that resembles a dinosaur. In fact, scientists believe the Komodo dragon has survived unchanged since the time of the dinosaurs, millions of years ago. Its only wild habitat is six small, isolated islands in the Java Sea, in Indonesia. The lizard is named after one of the islands, Komodo.

For many years, explorers brought home stories of these scary creatures. Then, in the early twentieth century, two pearl fishermen checked out the rumors and reported to a museum director in Java that these dragons actually did exist. The museum director sent an expedition to capture the first live specimens.

An adult Komodo dragon, the world's largest lizard, measures about ten feet long and weighs two to three hundred pounds. It has sharp, backward-curving teeth, sharp claws on its short legs, and loose, leathery skin with tough scales. The female lays eggs about the size of baseballs, and the hatchlings are about twenty-one inches long.

A Komodo eats carrion, which is the flesh of dead animals. It can kill its own prey if it has to—pigs, rats, goats, and small deer—and can knock

National Zoo, Smithsonian Institution / Jessie Cohen

Among the lizards that have survived from the age of dinosaurs is the rare, ten-foot-long Komodo dragon.

down a large animal with one swat of its long, heavy tail. But because it isn't especially fast on its short legs and has to rely on surprise attacks, it prefers to dine on animals that are already dead.

At a zoo, you may see other lizards called dragons as well as various types of ferocious-looking lizards known as monitors. The Komodo dragon is technically an extremely rare monitor. If you get a chance to visit the National Zoo in Washington, D.C., be sure to take a look at this remarkable lizard.

———

In describing the animals of hot, dry, rocky habitats, it would be hard to overlook the **desert tarantula**, one of a vast group of living creatures called invertebrates, animals that don't have backbones.

If someone asked you what kinds of animals exist in the greatest number on earth, what would you say? Mammals, such as human beings, dogs, cats, monkeys, and hoofed animals? Or would you say birds? Or fish? All would be the wrong answer. Those creatures put together make up only about 1 percent of the living creatures on earth! Over 90 percent are invertebrates. Insects, spiders, worms, and sea creatures such as crabs and clams are among the millions of different kinds of invertebrates.

Tarantulas have a bad reputation, which they don't deserve. People think they are poisonous and try to kill them, but in truth, most kinds of tarantulas are quite mild-tempered except when pursuing mates or food. In the unlikely event that one does bite a human, its bite hurts about as much as a bee sting and is not poisonous.

In the Middle Ages in a town called Taranto, in Italy, there was a superstition that the bite of a certain spider was venomous. People who were bitten would do a whirling dance that they believed would sweat the poison out of their bodies. The dance became known as the tarantella, after Taranto, and the folklore about the poisonous spider became confused with the tarantula. That's the origin of people's exaggerated fear of the tarantula.

In the wild, the desert tarantula can be found in Arizona, New Mexico, and southern California. It lives underground and only emerges at night to hunt for its prey—insects, lizards, sometimes small mice and birds. Male tarantulas usually die within a year after mating, but females are thought to live up to twenty years in the wild, and as long as thirty years in captivity.

Arizona-Sonora Desert Museum

The desert tarantula is actually a quite harmless spider and does not deserve its bad reputation.

Some people like to keep these spiders, especially pretty ones, as pets in vivariums or terrariums. A tarantula is not particularly responsive, but it is interesting.

In zoos, tarantulas are usually displayed in dioramas—naturalistic displays behind glass. Because these spiders are gentle creatures, zoo employees sometimes use them in educational events and demonstrations. Many children are fascinated by these big, fuzzy spiders.

Animals of the Woodlands

The world's woodlands and forests can vary greatly, depending on temperature, rainfall, wind, and the shape of the land. Some woodlands grow along the coasts, some high in the mountains, some along the borders of grasslands. Each has different types of trees and vegetation. Every continent except Antarctica has some type of woodlands.

Because forests are so different, animals that live within them also vary greatly. Some live mostly in the trees and, like koalas, for instance, have long, curved claws that help them cling to the branches and also dig up bark and roots. Others, like lemurs, have hands; still others live on the ground and are browsers—animals who nibble on leaves, mosses, berries, and other forest vegetation. Many have protective brown, gray, or striped coloring that blends in with the shadows of the forest and helps to hide them from predators, which also, in the balance of nature, live there.

In many zoos, you will see woodland animals confined in small cages with dirt or concrete floors and empty of anything except perhaps a shelf, rock, or tree trunk.

However, the best zoos have them in natural exhibits. Some animals may be sitting high up in the trees or stretched out along a limb. Others may be resting on the ground under the trees. Sometimes their natural camouflage makes them hard to see. One of the adventures in visiting a zoo with good exhibits of woodland animals is searching for and spotting the animals in or among the trees.

––––––––

Koalas are so slow moving you probably won't have trouble spotting one in a zoo. Though it looks like a teddy bear, the koala is not a bear at all. It is a marsupial, a mammal of which the female has a pouch or pocket on

The gentle koala looks like a huggable teddy bear but is not a bear at all.

her belly. A baby koala is less than one inch long when it's born and not fully developed, so it crawls into its mother's cozy pouch. There it nurses and grows for six months, at which time it is about six inches long and can live outside. Koalas, kangaroos, and opossums are marsupials.

The only place you'll find koalas in the wild is in the forests of Australia. Because they are timid and gentle animals, they were easily hunted and killed for many centuries for their soft fur. They almost became extinct. Now, however, it is against the law to kill them.

The original Australian native people gave koalas their name—it means "no drink," because the animals drink hardly any water. They get enough moisture from the leaves of the eucalyptus plant, which is the only food they eat. They must have fresh leaves every day, so in order to exhibit koalas, a zoo must grow its own eucalyptus, which needs a warm climate, or else ship the plants in every few days by plane.

When we hear the word *panda*, most of us think of the giant panda, the black-and-white, bearlike animal from China. The little red panda was formerly called the lesser panda, but now scientists have decided it is actually more like a raccoon than simply a scaled-down giant panda.

When you see a red panda in a zoo, it will most likely be lounging or sleeping in the trees. Sometimes it stretches out and drapes itself along a branch with its legs hanging down, or it curls up in a ball and sleeps with its tail wrapped around its head. Or maybe all you'll see of it is a little face peering out from the leaves.

In the wild, the red panda lives in a long, narrow habitat within the bamboo forests of the Himalayan Mountains. Though it eats birds, eggs, rodents, and insects, this animal's main food is bamboo shoots. But human settlements are pushing the red panda farther up into the mountains where there is no bamboo, and so it has become seriously endangered in the wild.

In the Species Survival Plan, scientists are studying the red panda closely in zoos. They hope to learn enough about its habits, especially its reproduction, to keep it from becoming extinct. The National Zoo is a leader in the study of the red panda.

Cincinnati Zoo/Ron Austing

A short-legged little animal about the size of a raccoon, the red panda is seriously endangered in its bamboo forest habitat.

The scientific word *primate* refers to certain animals that have hands and large brains, among other characteristics. The family of primates includes humans, apes, monkeys, and lemurs. One primate, the Japanese macaque (pronounced ma-*kack*), lives in the lowland and mountain forests of Japan, though its range is shrinking as cities and other developments expand. Because it can endure temperatures well below freezing, it is also called the snow monkey. When it has on its thick coat of winter fur, its face peers out as if from a parka hood.

Japanese macaques live in troops that can range from ten to eight hundred animals. The leader is an adult male who directs the movement and defense of the troop. Interestingly, he derives his status not from being the biggest, oldest, or most aggressive, but by being the son of a female with very high status. Other sons of high-ranking females stay within the troop

There is no way a macaque, or any animal, can lead a normal life in a cage that's a prison.

and help maintain order. Those males with not such high status live on the outskirts of the troop or leave to join other troops.

The females stay all their lives in the troop in which they were born. They form a strong sisterhood, for they defend, groom, and play with not only the youngsters but also one another. At a good zoo with a troop of Japanese macaques, it's fun to watch the animals and figure out their relationships. If there are babies, in just a few minutes you can easily spot their mothers. Mothers who are relaxed, self-confident, and playful are likely to have infants with those qualities. When a mother is teaching her baby to walk, she sets it on the ground, backs away, and smacks her lips to encourage it to come to her.

Japanese macaques are among the most intelligent of primates. In captivity, they need trees to climb, rocks to perch on or hide among. Instead of dumping their food in one spot on the ground, a keeper may scatter it around in different places so that the animals can search for it the way they forage for food in the wild. They can get away from one another to eat in peace so the greedy ones don't steal from the slow eaters.

Lemurs (pronounced lee-mur) are also primates, related to monkeys and to the earliest ancestors of human beings. There are twenty different species, ranging in size from ten to twenty inches long, not counting their tails. **Ring-tailed lemurs** use their long striped tails for balancing.

Since prehistoric times, lemurs have lived on the huge island of Madagascar, and that is still the only place where they exist in the wild. There are

These Japanese macaques live in an open zoo habitat in a northern climate
that is natural for them.

a few reserves in Madagascar where lemurs are protected. Unfortunately,
however, the island is falling victim to rapid development—over three-
fourths of its lush forests have already been cut down. Most of the people of
Madagascar are very poor, and in trying to eke out a living they are
devastating their land. As the trees go, so do the lemurs, among other
wildlife. Many species of lemur are already extinct.

In their natural habitat, lemurs live in groups of up to fifty members in
which the females are boss. The animals feed together on a diet of fruit,
vegetation, berries, mushrooms, and insects. They warn one another of
predators and band together if they have to fight. They communicate with
mews, barks, howls, grunts, moans, clicks, and even purrs.

Lemurs are most active in the very early morning. The word *lemur* means
ghost, because as the animals move quietly through the trees in the dim
light, the native people thought they looked like ghosts.

Fortunately, ring-tailed lemurs do well in zoos, and many zoos have
them. In the better zoos, they are kept in woodsy enclosures with trees or

Lemurs like this ring-tailed are losing their native homes as Madagascar's forests are cut down.

artificial structures they can climb. At the Phoenix Zoo, for example, eight lemurs share a rather large forested island.

———

The ocelot, which once inhabited the dense thickets and dry bushlands of remote areas of Central America, Mexico, and the southwestern United States, is a well camouflaged animal. It has been trapped and hunted so that its handsome pelt could be used to make fashionable, high-priced coats. Now, ocelots are protected by law in some of their homelands, and it is illegal to bring ocelot skins into the United States.

Even so, ocelots in the wild are so rare and secretive that they are almost never seen. They hide during the day and come out only at night to hunt for food—mice, rabbits, birds, fish, and reptiles, especially snakes.

Decent zoos in warm climates keep ocelots in open-air enclosures that duplicate their semitropical homes and provide hiding places for them. Inferior zoos keep these wild cats in bare cages where they have no privacy. You might have come across an ocelot suffering in some traveling animal exhibit. Sometimes local authorities close down such exhibits, but the owners simply pack up their animals and move on.

Ocelots have also been sold in pet stores. Especially when they are young, they look adorable and cuddly, and sometimes mew like kittens. But they grow up to be nervous, strong, destructive animals. People should never try to keep animals of any wild species as pets.

Many of the wild cats breed easily in captivity, and the cubs are what might be called crowd pleasers, bringing the public, and money, to the zoos. But the better zoos control their breeding so as not to produce surplus cubs.

This terrified serval, a wild cat, could be sold at an animal auction to a roadside zoo, private collector, or hunting ranch.

Arizona-Sonora Desert Museum/Jack Dykinga

Instead of pacing in a bare cage, this ocelot plays in an enclosure that's
like its natural bushland home.

With some cats, zoos can use birth control implants with the females. These
implants, little capsules placed under the animals' skin, prevent them from
becoming pregnant. Whatever zoos do to control the breeding of most of
the wild cats is a kindness, in the long run, since cubs that would result
from their mating might end up in the hands of animal dealers.

———

Many kinds of bears are woodland animals, and they vary greatly in size.
The Alaskan brown bear, for instance, stands eight to twelve feet tall and
can weigh as much as sixteen hundred pounds. Smallest of all the bears is
the Malayan sun bear, named for the crest of gold hair on its chest. It
weighs only about a hundred and fifty pounds and is as tall at the shoulder as a very big dog.

This bear lives in the forests of Southeast Asia—Malay, Burma, Thai-
land, Sumatra, and parts of India. An expert tree climber, it builds a nest for

The golden crest on its chest gave the little Malayan sun bear its name.

itself high in the trees and spends most of the day there, resting and sunbathing. At night, it climbs down to search for food. Its diet is fruit, vegetables, roots, palm shoots, insects, and whatever small animals it can catch. It uses its long, sharp, curved claws to dig for roots and pry open logs for insects, or to obtain one of its favorite foods—honey. Intelligent and retiring, this bear will, however, defend itself fiercely when molested.

Like so many forest animals, the Malayan sun bear is losing its habitat. It is also hunted by some Asian people and is an endangered species.

Many zoos exhibit these little bears, usually in open habitats with rocks and trees or climbing structures. In the wild, they are solitary by nature, joining up with mates only at breeding time, but at a zoo, a male may share a habitat with females during the day but have his own place to eat and sleep. During the breeding season, the better zoos may keep the male by himself, so as to prevent the birth of too many cubs.

Animals of the Rain Forests

Tropical rain forests, or jungles, cover a large part of the earth—vast parts of South America, Mexico, Africa, Asia, and Hawaii. They have, as their name implies, a great deal of rainfall and a warm climate.

More species of plants and animals live in the rain forests than in all other ecosystems combined. Yet this is the ecosystem that is most endangered; one hundred acres of the world's rain forests are being destroyed every minute of every day, year-round. People are cutting down the trees for wood, they are burning the land to clear it for farming and ranching. With the forests go not only the wildlife that lives in them but plants and trees that give useful products such as rubber, chocolate, and most important, medicines. Furthermore, rain forests play an important role in the climate of the entire earth, and removing them upsets the earth's atmosphere and contributes to the greenhouse effect. This is a gradual, dangerous warming of the earth's atmosphere caused by pollution. The destruction of the rain forests is one of the biggest dangers to the future of all life on earth.

Ironically, clearing rain forest trees to create farmland and pasture is a foolish thing for the farmers and ranchers to do because rain forest soil has very limited nourishment. When the trees are removed, the soil gradually becomes hard and nothing will grow in it. The richness of this ecosystem is in the forest canopy—the tops of the trees, which are very tall and have broad leaves. Many of the animals, including monkeys, never come down to the ground at all but live entirely in the canopy.

A number of the best zoos have built very creative and beautiful rain forest exhibits, such as Jungle World at the Bronx Zoo and Tropic World at the Brookfield Zoo, with clouds, waterfalls and pools, trees, vines, and animals living in almost complete ecosystems.

———

The golden lion tamarin monkey is one victim of rain forest destruction. It is found only in Brazil. Probably no more than 150 are left in the wild, and the species would soon have disappeared forever except for the zoos working to save it through the Species Survival Plan.

In a golden lion tamarin family, the father carries his twin youngsters on his back.

This monkey is also called golden-headed tamarin or simply lion tamarin. Despite its golden mane, it's a small monkey, about the size of a squirrel. Females are even smaller than the males. Newborn baby tamarins, almost always twins, ride on their mother's back. But after about a week, they are too heavy for her to carry, so the father takes over. They are the only primates besides humans in which the father actively helps in caring for his young. These monkeys in fact mate for life and always live in family groups.

As their population in zoos has increased, some have been released, a few small groups at a time, into a twelve-thousand-acre park in Brazil where they are protected. The monkeys can't go directly from zoos into the wild. Tamarins at the National Zoo, for example, were released from their cages into the trees on the zoo grounds, but sleeping nests and food were provided. At first, the food was tied in bundles and left in plain sight; then the food bundles were hidden among the leaves so the monkeys had to search for them. After that, the monkeys were taken to Brazil and lived at a sort of halfway house before they were released into the rain forest.

Not all the zoo-born golden lion tamarins that have been released have survived. But unless their rain forest is destroyed, enough of them have made the transition from captivity to freedom to give hope that returning these highly endangered monkeys to the wild is an idea that will work.

––––––

Largest of all the primates is the **gorilla**, an ape. Female gorillas generally weigh two to three hundred pounds; an adult male gorilla might stand six feet tall and weigh as much as five hundred pounds.

King Kong is an imaginary creature. Though they are very powerful, gorillas are actually shy, quiet, mild-mannered, and exclusively vegetarian. When threatened, males stand up and beat their chests and make a lot of noise. This looks scary, but it is usually only bluff—a gorilla will fight only to defend himself or a member of his troop.

Gorillas live in the mountain or lowland rain forests of Africa. They are highly social and live in troops, never alone. Typically, a troop will be

This gorilla baby, six hours old, lives with its family in the forestlike zoo habitat where it was born.

headed by an older male with gray hair, called a silverback, and include several females and youngsters of different ages. In the past, it was common for a zoo to keep a gorilla by itself, in a bare concrete cage. Today, only the worst zoos inflict that kind of suffering on this intelligent, social animal.

Both the mountain and the lowland gorillas are severely endangered. Loss of their rain forest habitat is one reason. Another is that poachers capture infant gorillas to sell to anybody who'll buy them. To capture a baby, hunters have to shoot the mother and often others who try to defend the baby. Zoos in Europe and Mexico have been known to buy gorilla babies illegally, which encourages poachers. AAZPA zoos do not buy animals that are suspected to come from poachers.

The Woodland Park Zoo was one of the first to get its gorillas out of cages and into a natural habitat. Some other zoos are doing the same. The story of one zoo's animal, Willie B, is a good example. When he was an infant, Willie B had been torn from his mother in the wild, put in a box, shipped to the United States, and eventually sold to the Atlanta Zoo. He was put in an indoor cage like a prison cell, and there he stayed for twenty-seven years.

Then, a few years ago, a new administrator was hired to rebuild the Zoo Atlanta, as it is now called. The first thing he did was to raise several million dollars to create a large, forested outdoor habitat for Willie B. On the day the habitat was complete, Willie B, who was by now a silverback, stepped cautiously out into the fresh air and sunshine for the first time in his adult life. He was dumbstruck with wonder. He looked at the sky, touched the grass, walked up to a tree and felt the leaves. He has chosen to be outdoors most of the time ever since. Life became even better for him when two females were introduced into his habitat to keep him company.

———

Among the other animals hard hit by rain forest destruction are the fruit bats, a large group of bats that eat fruit and flowers. These bats, like bees, are essential in propagating certain fruit trees and flowers. As they eat, they spill or eliminate seeds onto the ground, where the seeds take root. But in some places people eat fruit bats, and sometimes farmers kill them, thinking they are pests.

There are as many as eight hundred different species of bats, living all over the world in trees, caves, and under the eaves of houses. Many people dislike them and consider them very ugly, even frightening, creatures associated with haunted houses and cemeteries. But most bats are harmless and in fact do a lot of good. The insect-eating species, for example, are the only predators of night-flying insects such as mosquitoes.

Bats are not birds but mammals. They are the only mammals that fly, and they have both legs and wings. In size, they range from those with wingspans of about seven inches to the flying foxes, with wingspans of four feet. Bats are furry except for their wings, which are covered with leathery skin.

They spend a lot of time cleaning themselves, like cats. Their favorite position for sleeping is hanging upside down.

Most kinds of bats are active at night, using their highly efficient sonar to guide them as they fly. However, if you've heard the expression "blind as a bat," that's inaccurate—bats are not blind and in fact some species are day flyers and get around without sonar. Flying foxes, for example, rely on their vision and sense of smell.

Flying foxes, obviously named for their little foxlike faces, are natives of the rain forests of Madagascar, India, Southeast Asia, and the islands of the Indian Ocean. They roost in large colonies in trees, and are strong, swift flyers. A baby clings to its mother's body even when she's in flight.

Riverbanks Zoo

A flying fox, one of many varieties of fruit-eating bats, helps to propagate forest trees and flowers.

Many zoos have bats in naturalistic, darkened habitats behind glass, where you can watch them flying about. However, you are more likely to see fruit bats, including flying foxes, in daylight in rain forest exhibits.

———

Rain forests are home to thousands of species of birds, including many of the world's most colorful. The hyacinth macaw is a good example; its deep rich color resembles the blue hyacinths of spring.

Macaws are members of the parrot family, and while there are many, many types of parrots that live in tropical or semitropical areas around the

Riverbanks Zoo

The hyacinth macaw is losing its wild home, the disappearing rain forest of Brazil.

world, the hyacinth macaw is rare and found only in the disappearing rain forests of Brazil. It is a big bird, almost three feet long from beak to tail, and has a big voice too—a loud, harsh squawk. In the wild, it lives in pairs or small groups.

In captivity, hyacinth macaws are usually quite gentle with their keepers. They need a lot of space to fly in and should be kept only in large aviaries, never in cages. These birds don't breed readily in captivity, but a few zoos have bred them successfully. The chicks hatch naked and blind and must be fed partially digested food by both parents.

Some people like to keep macaws as pets, and because they are expensive, there is a brisk business in poaching them. Many birds die during capture. Those that survive are crammed into tiny boxes and concealed in planes or trucks, so many more suffocate or die of stress during transport. Survivors are smuggled into this country to bird dealers and pet stores. Humane and environmental organizations ask bird lovers to buy only captive-bred birds such as budgies and canaries, but not *any* parrots or other exotic birds, because this encourages poaching and smuggling.

A good zoo will not buy any bird that it suspects has been obtained by poaching. Also, when the United States Customs Inspectors catch a shipment of illegal wild birds, they confiscate the birds from the smugglers and call the AAZPA to find suitable zoos that would like to have them.

46

The gecko lizards, 660 known species of them, are found in all the warm climates of the world. They are harmless to human beings, and in fact, are a benefit because they eat insects, especially mosquitoes. Geckos are nocturnal, active at night rather than during the day. They're also vocal, squeaking and chattering—in fact, they probably got their name from one of their calls: "gecko, gecko."

These lizards can skittle up vertical surfaces, such as trees and walls; they can even walk upside down with no problem. Also, like many lizards, they have regenerative tails. That means that when a gecko loses its tail to a predator or for any other reason, it will grow another.

Most geckos are six to eight inches long, but the **tokay gecko**, the largest species, measures up to fourteen. It is also one of the handsomest. Its habitat is the warm, moist areas of Southeast Asia. The people of Malay, who gave the lizard its name, *toke*, believe it brings good luck. If a tokay gecko takes up residence after people have moved into a new house, or upon the birth of a new baby, it is welcomed.

Many zoos have geckos, including the tokay, because they are relatively easy to display. They are usually kept in simple enclosures or indoor vivariums, with rocks and tree limbs and greenery. Sometimes when you try to find one in an exhibit, you may look and look before you spot it, motionless and blending in with the scenery, right in front of your eyes.

Gladys Porter Zoo

A handsome foot-long lizard of Southeast Asia, the tokay gecko is thought to bring good luck.

Gladys Porter Zoo

Very few of the world's snakes are venomous, but the colorful black-necked spitting cobra definitely is.

An African rain forest reptile that zoos exhibit behind glass is the handsome and very dangerous **black-necked spitting cobra**. It is the most common spitting cobra, about five feet long, and when threatened can raise up the front part of its body and spread its neck into a wide, flat hood.

As its name suggests, this carnivorous snake defends itself and kills its prey by spitting a toxic venom, which is stored in two glands in its cheeks. It spits the venom in a thin stream through its fangs, and its aim is so accurate it can hit a victim six feet away. The snake aims for the face, especially the eyes, and the venom can cause intense pain and temporary or even permanent blindness. Its main diet is small mammals and frogs.

If you ask how venomous snakes such as cobras are kept in zoos, the answer is *very carefully!* The doors to their terrariums are locked; a keeper must get a key to enter. A sign on the door warns of the danger, and includes a list telling what type of snake and how many are inside. That way, the keeper doesn't forget what he's dealing with and knows to be extremely cautious. Habitats with poisonous snakes also have alarms, so if a keeper does get bitten, he or she can summon help quickly.

In fact, when keepers enter the enclosure of any dangerous animals to feed them and clean their habitat, the keepers usually go in pairs—one person to keep his or her eyes on the animals every minute, while the other person services the enclosure.

The **okapi**, a hoofed mammal, is one of the most unusual and little known of all rain forest animals. It looks as if it's been put together wrong! From the front, it resembles a handsome purplish-brown giraffe. But its hindquarters and legs are striped, as if it had zebra shorts and socks on.

The okapi is actually a relative of the giraffe, but nowhere near as big. It's only about seven or eight feet tall, whereas a giraffe can be as tall as nineteen feet. The okapi's tongue, however, is so long this animal can use it to wash its own ears and eyes.

Its habitat is the rain forests of western Africa, in areas so remote and dense that the animal wasn't even discovered by explorers until

Dallas Zoo

Looking like a cross between a zebra and a giraffe, the rare okapi is being bred at cooperating zoos in the Species Survival Plan.

early in this century. The shy and quiet okapi lives in pairs, small family groups, or alone, and browses on vegetation and fruit.

To help this rare animal survive in the wild, a national park is being created, with the help of the World Wildlife Fund, in the large rain forest of Zaire. Named the Okapi National Park, it is intended to become a refuge for many species of rain forest animals.

At present, there are fewer than a hundred okapis in the world's zoos, several of which are cooperating in breeding them in the Species Survival Plan. The zoos keep okapis in pasturelike enclosures that may have relatively few trees. Not only would the animals eat the trees, but if spooked, might panic and run into them and hurt themselves. The fewer obstructions, the better, say the zoo people in charge of these valuable animals.

Animals of the Tundras and Taigas

The vast Arctic plains of North America, Europe, and Asia, and the tops of the very highest mountains everywhere, are called tundra. In the tundra, temperatures are above zero for only a couple of months out of the year. No trees and only a few plants can grow there.

The taiga is forested with pines and other coniferous trees. It has snow all winter, and many lakes and marshes. This type of ecosystem is found in the Soviet Union, Scandinavia, and North America.

Not many animals and birds are able to live in the tundra and taiga, but some do. Since most icy waters contain fish, many of the northern animals are fishers, and some are predators who live on whatever animals and birds they can find. A few herbivores exist on the sparse vegetation.

Some animals of these regions can adapt to temperate climates and are kept in all but the most southern zoos. Others are usually found in zoos in northern climates.

One carnivore, the **snow leopard**, is disappearing in its homeland, the highest and coldest altitudes of the Himalaya Mountains. Conservationists estimate that there are only about eight hundred left in scattered places in the wild. Even though the animals are now protected in Nepal and Tibet,

The snow leopard has been hunted almost to extinction for its beautiful coat.

they are still killed secretly by poachers because their skins, or pelts, bring big money. The pelts are smuggled into countries worldwide to be made into fashionable and expensive fur coats. Also, Mongolia allows some snow leopards to be shot by wealthy sport hunters.

This magnificent cat weighs about a hundred pounds and can easily leap thirty feet. Its footpads are covered with thick fur so it can glide across the snow. When it curls up to sleep, it may wrap its long tail around itself like a muffler. But little is known about its habits in the wild. It apparently survives on wild sheep and goats, deer, and marmots.

Though many wild cats are solitary, males and females joining up only to mate, in zoos snow leopards seem to be fairly social, getting along comfortably with others of their own kind. Zoo scientists also believe they may be monogamous. Males seem inclined to take part in raising the young, which is highly unusual among the big cats.

At present, there are some four hundred snow leopards in captivity in North America; many zoos now have at least two. However, their breeding is regulated by the Species Survival Plan.

Because the survival of snow leopards in the wild is so uncertain, there are no plans right now to release any from zoos. The goal of zoos breeding snow leopards in the SSP is to maintain their population at a certain level, with few annual increases or decreases.

———

Another wily predator, the wolf, also survives in some of the world's north-ernmost regions. People used to believe a lot of nonsense about wolves. They were thought to be evil killers who ate children like Little Red Riding Hood. There are legends about packs of them chasing horsedrawn sleighs through snowy forests long ago. And to this day, ranchers blame wolves for livestock losses far beyond reason.

As a result, throughout history wolves have been shot, poisoned, trapped, and burned alive in their dens. They are hunted on foot and from vehicles, by snowmobiles and from helicopters. Few other species are so relentlessly slaughtered. Wolves once ranged over much of the world and almost all of North America. Today, many kinds of wolves are already extinct, but they are still legally hunted in many places.

Humane Society of the United States/Herbet

Wolves in a small cage at a roadside zoo in Pennsylvania always search for a way out.

People believe a lot of nonsense about wolves, and seem to either love them
or hate them, including the rare Arctic variety.

The handsome Arctic wolf is a color variation of the gray wolf. The gray
wolf is rare, and the white or Arctic variation even rarer. The gray wolf is
protected in forty-eight states, and only a little over three hundred of them
live in captivity. The Arctic wolves here are among several at the Milwaukee County Zoo.

Wolves are efficient predators, and to feed themselves they kill the same
animals that people like to kill—mainly deer, elk, and caribou. While hunters aim for the best animals, wolves choose the old, injured, or sick, which
are easier to catch, leaving the strongest specimens to breed. Because they
usually prey on large animals, the only way wolves can get food is by joining forces. So they hunt in packs using clever strategy.

They also kill livestock when they have to. Since ranchers pasture their
sheep over great distances and don't employ shepherds, it should be no
surprise when occasionally a sheep is taken by a hungry predator.

Wolves are generally peaceful animals, rarely quarreling with their own kind. They call to one another over great distances. Highly social animals, they live in packs of from three or four up to perhaps twenty-four members. They mate for life and are devoted to their offspring; a wolf who is hunting is often searching for food not just for himself but to bring home to his mate and pups. Pack members share in taking care of the pups.

One problem wolves and other predators have in captivity is boredom. No matter how comfortable and natural their zoo habitat may be, most predator animals don't have enough to do. In the wild, their major activity is hunting for food, sometimes over long distances. In a zoo, they are of course fed, which leaves them with limited ways to expend their energy.

One American species, the red wolf, is being bred at several zoos in the Species Survival Plan in an effort to prevent its extinction. Already, some animals from the large red wolf population at the Point Defiance Zoo have been released to the wild and are surviving in one of their former natural habitats in North Carolina.

––––––

For sheer survival persistence, few carnivores can match the **wolverine**. This animal's name suggests it is related to the wolves, and it looks rather like a small bear, but it is actually a member of the weasel family. It has a bad reputation. For one thing, it has a strong musky smell about it like that of the skunk. Also, it will never win any prizes for beauty. With a stocky, powerful body about three feet long and weighing more or less forty pounds, it's the strongest of all mammals for its size.

Because the wolverine has a large appetite and is very brave, it eats not only fish, frogs, and small mammals but will also take on creatures twice its size. It will drive a mountain lion or grizzly bear away from its prey. It is said to hide in trees and drop on an unwary victim's back. This animal does whatever it takes to survive in its taiga habitat where food is scarce.

The wolverine also eats carrion, the decaying flesh of dead animals. The carrion eaters, or scavengers, include coyotes, hyenas, eagles, and vultures, to name a few. They play an important role in helping to clean up the environment, but people generally regard carrion eaters with scorn.

The wolverine has learned to avoid humans so successfully that it is rarely seen in the wild and is difficult to shoot or trap. In one recent hunting season, only 700 were killed—compared to 115,000 pronghorns, 326,000 coyotes, and 600,000 mule deer. Over 148 *million* wild creatures were killed that year by sport hunters and government "damage control" hunters. Wild animals suffer not only hunger, predation, accidents, injuries, and natural disasters such as floods and fires but hunters and trappers too. It is a mistake to think that wildlife lives in a Garden of Eden!

Milwaukee County Zoo/M. A. Nepper

Not many people love the wolverine, a forty-pound tough-looking little animal, but it is a clever survivor.

People of the northern climates have a lot of fearsome legends about the wolverine. One is that it is an evil spirit, and if you look into its eyes, you'll go insane. (However, zookeepers who take care of wolverines have not found this to be true!) One thing some zookeepers claim is true, however—wolverines are clever escape artists. Zoos keep them in secure habitats with trees and artificial rockwork. They are often solitary in the wild, so a single wolverine in a zoo is not necessarily lonesome.

———

Among the birds that live mainly in tundra regions is the snowy owl. This elegant bird of prey stands about two feet tall, with a wingspan that can reach five feet. Because it has feathers on its legs and feet for warmth the snowy owl looks as if it's wearing pants. It uses its long, sharp talons in capturing the ground squirrels, rabbits, and especially the lemmings (small northern rodents) that make up its diet.

The snowy owl's usual habitat is the rolling tundra, coastal marshes, and beaches of the North Atlantic. However, in severe winters when prey becomes scarce, the owls have been seen as far south as Colorado, Utah, northern California, Pennsylvania, and even Long Island.

Because trees are scarce in the tundra, snowy owls are primarily ground dwellers. They don't hoot, but make a variety of trills and purrs. Also, unlike many owls, they hunt in the daytime instead of at night.

Though hunters consider snowy owls trophies and shoot them whenever possible, the birds have comparatively few other enemies. At this point, their populations in the wild are not threatened.

Many zoos keep snowy owls in pairs—a male and a female. They produce chicks quite willingly in captivity.

———

One large herbivore, the **musk ox**, manages to survive by nibbling on the sparse grasses and mosses of the tundra and taiga.

Many thousands of years ago, musk oxen roamed the frozen lands of Europe, Asia, and North America that circle the North Pole. They were plentiful, and prehistoric people killed them for their hides and meat. Then, in modern times came the explorers, hunters, and fur traders with

Pittsburgh Aviary/Mike Chikiris
The big snowy owl has feathered legs for warmth and like all owls is
a raptor, a bird of prey.

their high-powered guns. The Eskimos and Indians acquired guns too. By 1900, musk oxen were virtually extinct. They were saved only when conservationists established refuges for them in remote and frozen areas of Canada and Alaska, and more recently, in the Soviet Union.

Musk oxen are about the size of cows but look bigger because of their long, double-thick, woolly hair. Their Eskimo name is *oomingmak*, meaning the bearded one. They live in small or large herds.

When seriously threatened, a herd forms a tight circle, the adults shoulder to shoulder facing outward, the calves in the middle. Bravely facing their attackers, they

Minnesota Zoo

It's amazing that the musk ox, an animal the size of a cow, can find enough to eat in its cold, barren natural habitat.

use their big curving horns and can put up an excellent defense against all predators—except humans with guns. In parts of Alaska, it is now legal to hunt musk oxen. Sport hunters consider them great trophies, even though the animals are not difficult to find, are not dangerous, and are standing still—so easy to shoot a hunter can't miss.

A large herd of musk oxen, domesticated like sheep or cows, live on a farm in Alaska operated by the Oomingmak Cooperative. Every spring the animals shed their warm woolly undercoats, called qiviut (pronounced kiv-ee-ute). The wool is spun into soft yarn and sent to people in isolated Arctic villages, who knit warm scarves and sweaters to earn money.

With a few exceptions, the zoos that keep these shaggy animals are in northern climates suitable for them. In the zoos that have herds of musk oxen, calves are often born.

When You Go to a Zoo

Here's a checklist of things to look for and questions to ask:

1. Are the animals in exhibits that are appropriate for them? Remember that some species need space to run in, grass, and trees, while others need water to bathe or swim in, vines to swing on, or sand to dig in.

2. Does the zoo have its animals in large, comfortable, naturalistic habitats, even if that means limiting the number of different species?

3. Is the zoo accredited by the American Association of Zoological Parks and Aquariums? In general, an AAZPA zoo is likely to be a more interesting, humane, and enjoyable place than a non-AAZPA zoo.

4. Is the enclosure clean? If there is a pool or stream, is the water clean?

5. Are there places for the animals to hide if they want privacy? Do they have access to shade, shelter, and warmth if they need it?

6. Are the animals in proper social groupings—in pairs, herds, packs, colonies, families, or whatever would be normal for them in the wild? If an animal is by itself, is it an animal that is solitary by nature?

7. Are the animals protected, in enclosures beyond reach of people who might try to touch or bother them? Are people prevented from throwing litter into the habitats or coins into pools? If the animals are behind glass, is the window situated so people can't bang on it?

8. Do the animals seem relaxed and comfortable—or are they pacing incessantly or trying to escape from their enclosures?

9. Are there signs that give you information about the animals? Does the zoo offer lectures, classes, and education programs?

10. Do the animals have to do silly tricks to make the public laugh at them? Are they treated with respect, or are they made fun of?

Good Zoos To Visit

Many of the animals pictured or described in this book can be seen at the following zoos.

Arizona	Arizona-Sonora Desert Museum, Tucson
	Phoenix Zoo
California	Living Desert, Palm Desert
	Los Angles Zoo
Florida	Miami Metrozoo
Georgia	Zoo Atlanta
Illinois	Brookfield Zoo, Chicago
Louisiana	Audubon Zoo, New Orleans
Minnesota	Minnesota Zoo, Apple Valley
Missouri	St. Louis Zoo
New York	Bronx Zoo, New York City
	Central Park Zoo, New York City
Ohio	Cincinnati Zoo
Pennsylvania	Pittsburgh Aviary
South Carolina	Riverbanks Zoo, Columbia
Texas	Dallas Zoo
	Gladys Porter Zoo, Brownsville
Washington	Point Defiance Zoo and Aquarium, Tacoma
	Woodland Park Zoo, Seattle
Washington, D.C.	National Zoo, Smithsonian Institution
Wisconsin	Milwaukee County Zoo

Index

Page numbers in *italics* refer to photographs.